A Dragon
on the Doorstep

written by **Stella Blackstone**
Illustrated by **Debbie Harter**
Sung by **Fred Penner**

Barefoot Books
Step inside a story

www.barefootbooks.com

There's a dragon on the doorstep,
Do you think he wants to play?

Let's lock him in the cupboard,
Then let's run away!

There's a crocodile in the cupboard,
Don't go inside!

Let's put him in the attic,
Then run downstairs and hide!

There's a spider in the attic,
Quick! Get out of here!

Let's put him in the toy chest
And hope he'll disappear!

There's a tiger in the toy chest
With a very fierce glare!

Let's chase him to the bedroom
And tell him to stay in there!

There's a big bear in the bedroom,
With the most enormous paws!

Let's hide him in the laundry
And make sure we shut the doors!

There's a lion in the laundry,
Have a look and see!

Let's shut him in the garage
And lock it with the key!

There's a gorilla in the garage
And all the others too!

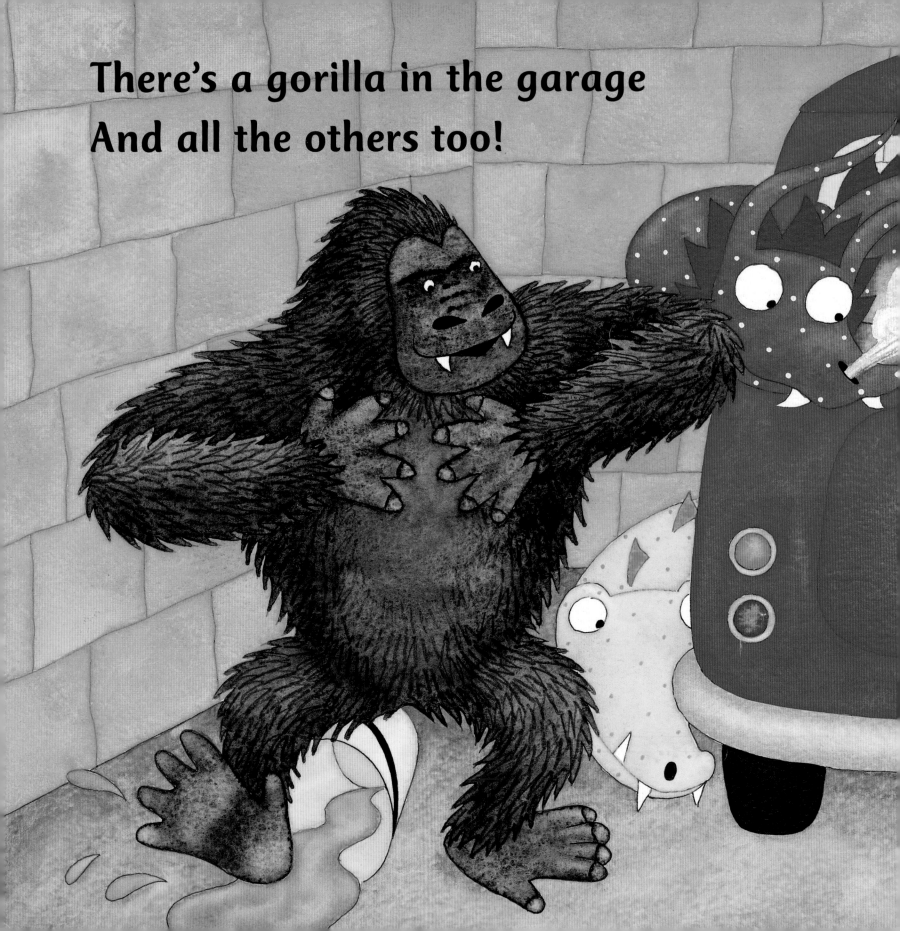

Everybody has escaped!
Watch out or they'll catch you!

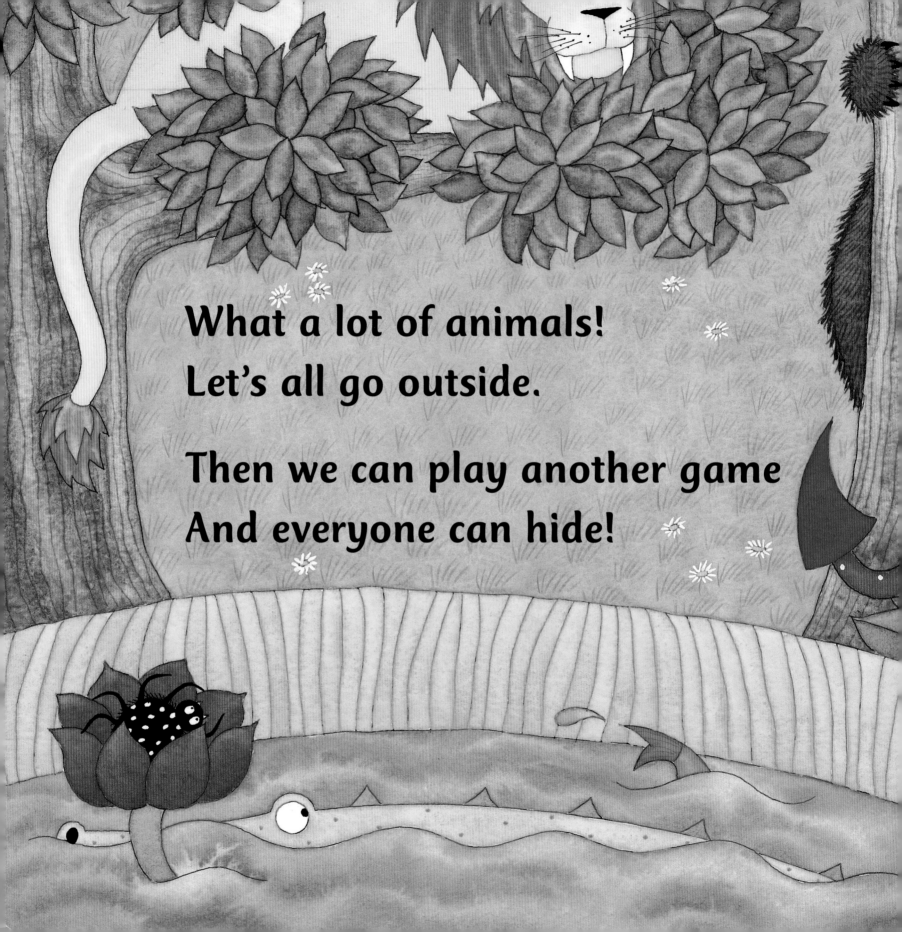

What a lot of animals!
Let's all go outside.

Then we can play another game
And everyone can hide!

For Sarah, with much love — S. B.
For Eva, Yoyo and Luke — D. H.

Barefoot Books
294 Banbury Road
Oxford, OX2 7ED

Barefoot Books
2067 Massachusetts Ave
Cambridge, MA 02140

Graphic design by Barefoot Books, England
Reproduction by Grafiscan, Verona
Printed in China on 100% acid-free paper
This book was typeset in Bokka and Mercurius Medium
The illustrations were prepared in watercolour, pen and ink, and crayon
on thick watercolour paper

ISBN 978-1-84686-826-9

British Cataloguing-in-Publication Data:
a catalogue record for this book is available from the British Library

Library of Congress Cataloging-in-Publication Data is available under
LCCN 2004028587

3 5 7 9 8 6 4